To my daughter, Heather Marie, and her imaginary childhood friends: Golly the dolly, Clown Baby, and Courtney Azalea Ker-shell. —R.T.

STERLING CHILDREN'S BOOKS
New York

An Imprint of Sterling Publishing
1166 Avenue of the Americas
New York, NY 10036

STERLING CHILDREN'S BOOKS and the distinctive Sterling Children's Books logo
are trademarks of Sterling Publishing Co., Inc.

Text and Illustrations © 2015 by Richard Torrey

ISBN 978-1-4549-1179-1

Distributed in Canada by Sterling Publishing
c/o Canadian Manda Group, 664 Annette Street
Toronto, Ontario, Canada M6S 2C8
Distributed in the United Kingdom by GMC Distribution Services
Castle Place, 166 High Street, Lewes, East Sussex, England BN7 1XU
Distributed in Australia by Capricorn Link (Australia) Pty. Ltd.
P.O. Box 704, Windsor, NSW 2756, Australia

The illustrations were created using oil base pencils, watercolor, and digital media.
Design by Andrea Miller

For information about custom editions, special sales, and premium and corporate purchases, please contact Sterling Special Sales at 800-805-5489 or specialsales@sterlingpublishing.com.

Manufactured in China
Lot #:
2 4 6 8 10 9 7 5 3 1
02/15

www.sterlingpublishing.com/kids

ALLY-SAURUS

& the First Day of School

by Richard Torrey

STERLING CHILDREN'S BOOKS
New York

"Time to wake up, sleepyhead," said Mother.
"My name is not sleepyhead, it's Ally-saurus!" said
a voice from beneath the covers.

"Very well, **ALLY-SAURUS**," said Mother. "We don't want to be late for your first day of school."

"**ROAR!**" said Ally-saurus.

Taking off her favorite dinosaur pajamas, Ally-saurus dressed in her brand-new first-day-of-school outfit.

"Your pants are on backward," said Father.

"That's so my dinosaur tail can stick out," explained Ally-saurus.

"Let's wear our pants the right way," said Father.

" ROAR! " said Ally-saurus.

She chomped her cinnamon toast with fierce teeth.

"There's no room for my stuffed dinosaurs!" said Ally-saurus as she packed her new dinosaur backpack.

"They'll be waiting for you when you get home," said Father.

"Do you think there will be other dinosaurs in my class?" asked Ally-saurus.

"I think you're going to make a lot of new friends," said Mother.

The teacher, Mrs. Woolhandler, stood at the classroom door greeting the new students.

"Are you Ally?" asked Mrs. Woolhandler.

"Yes, but you can call me Ally-saurus," said Ally-saurus.

"Wonderful," said Mrs. Woolhandler. "And you can call me Mrs. W."

At snack time, Ally-saurus chomped her grapes with fierce teeth.

"**ROAR!** This is how dinosaurs eat!"

The other children ate their snacks quietly.

Mrs. W's class worked hard all morning.

They made nameplates for their cubbies.

"I'm making a dinosaur!" said Ally-saurus.
"Are you making a dinosaur?"

"No," said Robert. "I'm making a spaceship."

They learned about the weather.

"That cloud looks like a dinosaur," said Ally-saurus.

"No, it looks like a castle!" insisted Lila.

"A castle for a *princess*!" said Tina.

"*Three* princesses!" added Kim, and they all giggled.

They learned about letters.

"Who can tell me a word that starts with the letter *A*?" said Mrs. W.

"*Dinosaur!*" roared Ally-saurus.

"*Dinosaur* starts with *D*," said Mrs. W.

"I know," said Ally-saurus. "I just like dinosaurs."

"I think everyone likes dinosaurs," said Mrs. W.

"Not as much as princesses!" said Tina.

Soon it was time for lunch.

"These seats are saved for princesses, not dinosaurs," said Tina.

"You're not a *real* princess!" roared Ally-saurus.

"You're not a *real* dinosaur," said Tina.

"Then why am I eating dinosaur food?" asked Ally-saurus.

"That's baloney!" said Tina, and the other princesses giggled.

Ally-saurus found a seat at an empty table. She thought about her stuffed dinosaurs back home and wished she could eat lunch with them.

"Is this seat being saved?" asked Cindy.

"No," said Ally-saurus, shaking her head.

"Can I sit here?" asked Jason.

"Yes," said Ally-saurus, sounding surprised.

"Is there room for me?" asked Walter.

"Of course!" said Ally-saurus.

"That's a nice dinosaur shirt," said Cindy.
"I like dinosaurs, and I also like dragons!"

"I like dragons and dinosaurs," said Jason.
"But I like lions the best!"

"And I *love* my new lunchbox!" said Walter.

Everyone giggled at that—even Ally-saurus.

Feeling much better, Ally-saurus began to chomp her sandwich with fierce teeth.

" ROAR! This is how dinosaurs eat!"

ROARRRRRRRRRR!

Soon the whole table was roaring and chomping.

When lunch was over, Mrs. W's class headed to the playground, where Ally-saurus ran with a lion (and Walter) . . .

. . . soared with a dragon (and Walter) . . .

. . . flew in a spaceship . . .

. . . and chased away a band of pirates (and Walter).

Ally-saurus even had tea with some grateful princesses.

And afterward, the princesses stomped and roared
through the jungle with Ally-saurus.

When the bell rang, Mrs. W. walked her class to the school library for the first time.

Each student was allowed to pick out a book to read at home that night.

"I'm going to find a story about lions!" roared Jason.

"I'm going to find a story about princesses," said Tina. "Or maybe pirates."

"I'm going to find a story about lunchboxes!" said Walter.

"I wonder if they have stories about dinosaurs," said Ally-saurus.

"We *do* have stories about dinosaurs," said the librarian. "And stories about cowboys, and pirates, and butterflies, and bunnies . . ."

A-L M-Z

The next morning, Ally hopped out of bed.

She couldn't wait to get to school.